HARRY I WAS?!

Patriots Point Institute of History, Science & Technology
Mt. Pleasant, SC

PATRIOTS POINT
★ HOME OF THE USS YORKTOWN ★

CONTENTS

THE GREAT DEPRESSION & WWII
As Told by Harold "Harry" Smith & William Franklin Smith

COLD WAR TO TODAY
As Told by William Franklin Smith & Benjamin Jackson Smith

MEDAL OF HONOR RECIPIENTS OF SOUTH CAROLINA

As of this date, 30 men from South Carolina have received our nation's highest military honor. Below are a few.

- ❖ Batesburg — William Kyle Carpenter (War on Terrorism)
- ❖ Beaufort — Middleton Elliot (Mexican Campaign)
- ❖ Charleston — Ralph Johnson (Vietnam War)
- ❖ Folly Island — William Henry Walling (Civil War)
- ❖ Greenville — Robert Sidney Kennemore (Korean War)
- ❖ Hendersonville — John Thomas Kennedy (Philippines)
- ❖ Sandy Springs — Freddie Stowers (WWI)
- ❖ Six Mile — Furman L. Smith (WWII)

An Army Medal of Honor from World War II
Courtesy of the Library of Congress

INTRODUCTION

M y name is Benjamin Jackson Smith. I am the great-great-grandson of Harold Scott Smith. His friends called him Harry. (Here is a picture of him in his Civil War uniform.)

Courtesy of the collection of Michael Welch

I only knew my great-great-grandpa for a mere seven years. But through his gift of storytelling, I grew to love American history. His eyewitness accounts (from growing up as a little boy in the Lowcountry to building bridges in Europe during the Second World War) were so clear. I felt as if I was right there with him.

My family is so blessed to have much of his life in letters, journals, and even old newspaper clippings he collected.

One of my favorite stories was the one about the day he met President Lincoln during the Civil War. He would be so proud that my daughter, Anne, (his great-great-great granddaughter) serves as a pilot aboard the aircraft carrier USS *Lincoln*!

Today would be my great-great-grandpa Harry's 102nd birthday. In his honor, and in remembrance of his favorite president, Lincoln, how many 'scores' did Harry live? To help you, a score is twenty years. (Editor's note: Score, as a measurement of time, was used in the opening line of President Lincoln's famous Gettysburg Address: "...Four score and seven years ago..."). If you guessed that Harry lived five scores, you're right.

$$(20 \times 5) + 2 = 102.$$

What I would like to do, through Harry's stories and my family letters, is take you on a journey through history. Together, we will explore his days as a young boy in South Carolina to my daughter serving our great country as a female fighter pilot. So, get your imaginations ready to go where NO STUDENT HAS GONE BEFORE!

(Individual Heritage Chart)

DESCENDENTS OF HAROLD "HARRY" SCOTT SMITH

Nancy Jean Smith (daughter)

William Smith (son)

Andrew Smith (grandson)

William Franklin Smith (great-grandson)

Benjamin Jackson Smith (great-great-grandson)

Anne Hutchinson Smith (great-great-great-granddaughter)

Courtesy of the collection of Michael Welch

CHAPTER 1 - YOUNG SOLDIER
By Harold Scott Smith

M y Pa was named Winfield Scott Smith and my Ma was Mary Caroline Fairbanks Smith. I grew up in Moncks Corner, South Carolina in a large cabin built on my Grandpa's farm beside a crystal blue stream. I was the baby of the family with 7 brothers and 2 sisters.

<u>Farm Life</u>

Life on a farm was hard. It took a lot of work to feed all of us. Our food was grown on the farm or hunted and fished from nearby streams. Back then some foods could last for a few days using methods such as drying, pickling, salting or smoking.

My grandpa told us about the old "ice box" system of keeping foods cool in window boxes or stored in bins buried in the ground. Eating spoiled food was a common cause of illness and even death, especially in summer. You could buy ice shipped from up North, but most ordinary folks like my family could not afford it.

Most of our food was eaten the same day it was picked or caught. Milk came straight from our cows to our cups! The first electric refrigerator was not invented until 1850, the same year I was born. But the first household refrigerator was not sold until 1912.

Wild animals were plentiful in those days and were easily trapped by our men. Sometimes we would see animals, but our guns would miss more than we were able to shoot. We didn't just eat the animals we caught but used their skins to make blankets, rugs, clothing, and caps to keep our heads from getting too much of our South Carolina sun. When my grandpa was a kid in colonial days, his shoes were made from animal skins tied to his muddy feet. Of course, my favorite foot covering was no shoes at all, walking barefoot through the woods. On my 21st birthday, I bought my first pair of rubber-sole shoes invented by a guy named Charles Goodyear!?

<u>The Woods</u>

Have you ever heard of Francis Marion? He was my pa's hero. Night after night, my pa would tell my brothers and me stories about General Marion's famous fighting style and his ability to disappear in the swamps around our farm. During the Revolutionary War, the British gave Marion his famous nickname, "Swamp Fox." My brothers and I often pretended to be part of his "army," with my sisters having to play the part of the British. Of course, my brothers and I always won.

When we kids were not playing war or building forts, we would look for arrowheads in the woods with my sisters. We were always on the lookout for wild animals and strangers passing through. One day we were surprised by a slave. He was real scared and told us not to tell anybody that we had seen him. He kept saying something about an "Underground Railroad" and his need to get to Charleston. There, he planned to hide on board a ship heading up north. Later that night when we told my pa what we had seen, he told us the man must have run away from a nearby plantation. We didn't have slaves and were glad that Pa kept our secret and let the man get away.

School Days

Our school had only one room. Depending on our chores, there were days when all of my brothers and sisters were going to school in the same room, being taught by the same teacher. We learned "reading, writing and ciphering (Math). There were few decorations in schools back then and no fieldtrips...except to the "outhouse". The outhouse was our bathroom. It was a little shed in the back with the box over a hole. (Some wealthier farms called plantations had what were called 2 or 3 seaters!) Making it to the

8th grade was as far as many of us made it back then...especially once the Civil War began.

The War

When the War Between the States started, I was 11 years old. The army let me enlist, or sign up, as a drummer. Men from my home town, including my Pa, were put together in a company which was a group of 100 men. There were 10 companies in a regiment. All the men in the regiment were from Berkeley County. Now you tell me, how many total men were in our regiment?

In the early days that summer, we did lots of marching through swamps, mud and up and down steep mounds of dirt and grass. One day, we were all put on a train for Virginia. The trip took all night, and when we got there, we could hear the sounds of guns, cannons and drums.

On the morning of June 30th, 1862, my company was ordered to take the lead in the battle. As the drummer, I was at the back of our company with all the other musicians. I don't remember much, but there was a lot of smoke and confusion. Everything happened so fast, that before I knew it, I was surrounded by a bunch of men in blue uniforms. I was told that I was a Prisoner of War. My pa later told me that after the battle, he spent a week looking for me.

As a musician and a kid, I was treated much nicer than many POWs. I was told that I could be released and work as a Union Army drummer if I signed an Oath of Allegiance to the United States. After giving it a lot of thought, I agreed.

That's how I met and became friends with a young Union Army drummer, Willie Johnston. He was from Vermont and had one uncle that fought alongside him in the Union Army, and another that fought for the South. Like me, Willie had a family that was on both sides of the war.

One day, Willie told me about what happened to him during a battle that's now called the Seven Days battle. During a retreat, many men in his regiment left their guns and supplies behind to lighten their load on the march. But Willie held on to his drum during the long, grueling march. When they got to Harrison's Landing, he was the only drummer boy who still had his drum and the only one to play the drum for the whole regiment!

His Division Commander was so impressed, he wrote Willie's story in his report. One never knows who may read your story. President Lincoln heard of Willie and his drum and suggested to Secretary of War Edwin Stanton that Willie be given a medal for his valor (bravery.) In Sept. 1863, at the age of 13, Willie was the second person to receive the Medal of Honor and the youngest ever.

LEADERSHIP PRINCIPLE - FACILITATOR

One who makes an action or process easier.

Willie Johnston was a **facilitator**. Though he was only 13, he had a professional approach to his job as drummer boy. He knew his drum was important for facilitating commands to the regiment, so he performed his job to the best of his ability even when others did not.

TRULY HISTORIC TRIVIA

- Did you know Stonewall Jackson was shot accidentally by his own men? His arm was removed to save his life, but he died about a week later. He's the only Confederate to have two graves - one for his arm and one for his body.
- Did you know jelly beans were given to Union soldiers during the Civil War?
- Did you know the man who invented refrigeration was a doctor from South Carolina - John Gorrie? In 1844, he built an ice-maker for air conditioning to cool patients with malaria and yellow fever in Florida.

CHAPTER 2 - THE GETTYSBURG ADDRESS
By Harold Scott Smith

I t was Lincoln's love of reading and writing that prepared him to become the man who would lead our country in some of our saddest days. He was also known for his sense of humor and storytelling style.

<u>Letter from Harold Scott Smith to His Mother</u>

November 19, 1863

Dear Ma,

It's been a cloudy and chilly morning. There are about 50,000 people in and around Gettysburg. Willie and I are excitedly awaiting the arrival of the President of these "divided" United States. He is coming to dedicate (set aside for a particular purpose or reason) this piece of land on which so many soldiers from the North and the South have given their lives. The town's people continue to go about their daily lives as if nothing has changed since those sad days in July. They seem to just accept that right in the middle of their once quiet little town is a cemetery where many Yanks and Rebs now rest together. Willie continues to be a drummer but I switched to the bugle. The Army needed buglers to play "TAPS" at the many battlefield funerals. (Editor's Note: "TAPS" is a song played at flag ceremonies and funerals, generally on a bugle or trumpet.) The sights and sounds of war are never erased from one's mind. Our eagerness for war has been forever changed after witnessing so many wounded or dying on the battlefields from injuries and disease. Thankfully, being musicians, Willie and I are usually at the back of the lines during the heavy fighting.

Suddenly, everyone paused as some famous speaker steps up quickly on to the platform. He is talking about the "Rebs," and has gone on and on for almost two hours now. Most of us feel sad for the loss of life no matter what side they fought on. We are all "brothers." We pray that all the states will be "joined" back again someday soon.

When President Lincoln stepped up to the podium, he looked weary and sad standing there in his dark suit. His blue-gray eyes seem to fear the emotions he has kept in his heart during these dark days of history. He looked over the crowd and took some wads of paper that he stored in his tall hat on top of his head. The following speech I will never forget.

"*Four score and seven years ago our fathers brought forth, on this continent, a new nation, conceived in liberty, and dedicated to the proposition that all men are created equal. Now we are engaged in a great civil war, testing whether that nation, or any nation so conceived, and so dedicated, can long endure. We are met on a great battle-field of that war. We have come to dedicate a portion of that field, as a final resting-place for those who here gave their lives, that that nation might live. It is altogether fitting and proper that we should do this. But, in a larger sense, we cannot dedicate, we cannot consecrate—we cannot hallow—this ground. The brave men, living and dead, who struggled here, have consecrated it far above our poor power to add or detract. The world will little note, nor long remember what we say here, but it can never forget what they did here. It is for us the living, rather, to be dedicated here to the unfinished work which they who fought here have thus far so nobly advanced. It is rather for us to be here dedicated to the great task remaining before us—that from these honored dead we take increased devotion to that cause for which they here have the last full measure of devotion—that we here highly resolve that these dead shall not have died in vain—that this nation, under God, shall have a new birth of freedom, and that government of the people, by the people, for the people, shall not perish from the earth.*"

When he finished and stepped off the platform, the President seemed to wipe tears from his eyes and then looked straight at Willie and me with a smile. He motioned to his guards and walked to us. He extended his hand and in his kind voice thanked us for our service as musicians. He asked if we had enough food and warm clothes. We told him we were fine. He removed his tall hat and took out a small wrinkled piece of paper. It's amazing how much paper he had in that hat! He quickly wrote something on it. With a smile he handed the note to Willie and said, "God bless you boys." Once the President was far enough away we opened the note and read it, "*By order of Abe Lincoln please assign these two musicians to my Presidential detail as soon as possible.*" WOW!!! We are excited beyond words.

Love,

Your son, Harry

LEADERSHIP PRINCIPLE - COMMUNICATOR

One who gets his/her point across effectively.

Abraham Lincoln was a great **communicator** when he gave his Gettysburg Address. He chose his words carefully. So his speech was clear, brief and to the point with no shouting or grand displays.

TRULY HISTORIC TRIVIA

- Did you know that Abraham Lincoln handwrote 5 copies of this shortest speech given by a President so far?

- Did you know the Gettysburg Address was only 3 minutes and 272 words long? The speech had about 1,196 characters. If Lincoln had sent it on Twitter, how many 'tweets' would it take to send it? (Hint: a tweet is limited to 140 characters.)

- Did you know that 1 civilian was killed at the Battle of Gettysburg on the morning of July 3, 1863? Mary Virginia "Jennie" Wade was at her sister's home making biscuits on Baltimore Street when a bullet passed through the two wooden doors and struck her heart. She was buried on July 4, 1863.

Courtesy of the Library of Congress

Lincoln's Second Inaugural Address

Saturday, March 4, 1865

CHAPTER 3 - THE WAR ENDS & WE LOSE A PRESIDENT
By Harold Scott Smith

O n March 4, 1865, Willie and I were standing on the East Steps of the Capitol with our drum and bugle softly playing with the President's Band. Thousands were gathered along the muddy Pennsylvania Avenue to hear and see the President. The dome of our new Capitol building had just been completed, even with the war going on. For us, it was a symbol that these United States would be joined again.

Our time serving the President continued to teach us more than we ever imagined. His kindness was amazing, and he treated us as if we were his own 'boys'. We often joined him for walks to the old Soldier's Home, a few miles from the White House. It was there that he and his family tried to get away from the continuous flow of visitors. He never seemed to think of his safety, which concerned his bodyguards.

Standing very straight, the President approached the platform at the East Portico of the Capitol to take the oath of office and give his second inaugural speech. He stopped for a moment to look at the crowd. He kindly smiled, took out his notes and spoke for the next few minutes.

"Fellow-Countrymen... With malice toward none; with charity for all; with firmness in the right, as God gives us to see the right, let us strive on to finish the work we are in; to bind up the nation's wounds; to care for him who shall have borne the battle, and for his widow, and his orphan -- to do all which may achieve and cherish a just, and a lasting peace, among ourselves, and with all nations."

Once the speech was over, we headed back to the White House where the First Family greeted guests. Willie and I were among the musicians selected to play some of his favorite songs inside the East Room. He always requested to hear the song 'The Battle Hymn of the Republic'. It was originally written as a Civil War anthem. The President often asked for the song to be played and even invited Julia Ward Howe to the White House to sing the song. (Editor's Note: Poet and abolitionist Julia Ward Howe wrote the verses during the early days of the Civil War at the nearby Willard Hotel.)

Just a few weeks later, the day that we had all been waiting for finally came – the end of the Civil War. But the celebrating didn't last long. Here is a letter I wrote to my mother about the joy we felt at the end of the war and the sadness of what happened next.

Letter from Harold Scott Smith to His Mother

April 9, 1865

Dear Ma,

There was great relief when the White House Messenger arrived with word that General Lee and General Grant met at Appomattox Courthouse in Virginia. Grant was happy to send the news that the fighting between North and South is over! Though many hard times lay ahead for the South, the terms of surrender were kind. The President announced to all present that he had no plans to punish the South but to bring peace back to the Union.

That night, Mrs. Lincoln asked the President if they might attend a local comedy at Ford's Theatre called "Our American Cousin." She was hoping it would give them a chance to be together and a nice change for them both. Just before time to get into the carriage, President Lincoln called Willie and me into his office. He asked if we had ever been to a play. We said, "No, Mr. President." From that tall hat of his, he pulled out two tickets and (with a sparkle in his eyes and a relaxed smile we hadn't seen before) he said, "See you at the play, boys!"

We got really great seats on the front row. To our right we could easily see the box seat where the Lincolns would be sitting. It had a red, white and blue draped bunting (patriotic cloth) hanging from it that added to the excitement of the evening. Within minutes, President and Mrs. Lincoln entered to cheers by those of us seated in the theater. President and Mrs. Lincoln waved, smiled and sat down. The play began and so did the laughter.

Suddenly, a man jumped from the Presidential Box as the President slumped over. Mrs. Lincoln's screaming and crying could be heard as the President's limp body was carried from the theater across the street to the Peterson Boarding House.

Two of the Presidential guards came immediately and got Willie and me. Since we were part of his Presidential Detail, they feared for our lives as well. We went in to the room, later known as the Clark room, to see him. The next morning our President, mentor and friend, Abraham Lincoln, took his last breath. On April 15, Edwin M. Stanton said softly, "Now he belongs to the ages."

Your son,

Harry

LEADERSHIP PRINCIPLE - MOTIVATOR

One who gives others a reason to act or perform a task.

Julia Ward Howe was a **motivator** when she inspired both soldiers and civilians with the 'Battle Hymn of the Republic'. She was also an abolitionist who motivated others to act against slavery.

TRULY HISTORIC TRIVIA

- Did you remember that the same Secretary of War that stood by Lincoln's bed as he died was also the same person Lincoln had present Willie Johnston, my best buddy, the Medal of Honor in September of 1863?

- Did you know that when John Wilkes Booth jumped from the Presidential Box after shooting President Lincoln, he broke his leg as he landed on the stage? Booth was still able to escape. He and 3 of his conspirators were captured 3 days later in Virginia. They were trying to escape to the south.

- Did you know that Ford's Theatre has a Lincoln Book Tower? The 'books' in the tower are made from fireproof bent aluminum. Exhibit designers printed the cover art directly onto the metal book 'jackets.' The tower features 205 real titles, most of which are currently in print.

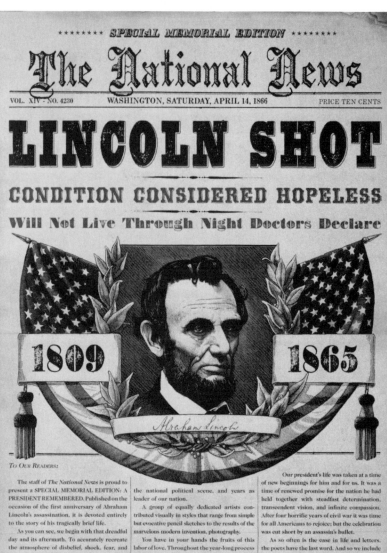

Courtesy of the Library of Congress

CHAPTER 4 – THE LONG RIDE HOME
By Harold Scott Smith

O n Friday, April 21, I remember following the coffin containing our President's body from the Capitol to a special funeral car waiting at the train depot. Six days had passed since our President was taken from us. He was the first President ever assassinated. Willie and I were part of the Presidential Honor Guard. Over 10,000 people in Washington, DC lined up to say 'goodbye' to our 16th President.

Mrs. Lincoln chose to have her husband buried in Oak Ridge Cemetery in his home town of Springfield, Illinois. She said he once told her he wanted a "quiet place for his burial." (Editor's Note: Oak Ridge Cemetery became the site of the Lincoln Tomb. See the photo on the next page.)

As sad as we were to lose our President, we were equally honored to be part of the military men chosen to guard his tomb. For the next year Willie and I were among a select group of musicians who played continuously outside the President's tomb.

The engine 'Nashville' of the Lincoln funeral train.
Courtesy of the Library of Congress

We often thought back to how he tried to keep our country together. His love of people was always visible regardless of the color of a soldier's uniform. I think President Lincoln's plan for reconstruction, or rebuilding, would have been much easier on the South if he had lived. His plan is summed up in his words, "with malice toward none, with charity toward all..." (Editor's Note: 'Malice' means wanting to hurt someone or see someone suffer.)

We were both almost 16 years old, and we had to grow up pretty fast because of the war. After our tour of duty, we planned to do some traveling. Here is a letter I received from my oldest brother Frank who lived in Kansas then.

Letter from Frank Smith to Harold Scott Smith

October 1867

Dear Harry,

The family and I are excited to have you coming to live with us and work in the candy store. You will be amazed at how many different types of candies there are since we were kids. There is also a nice young lady named Kathleen that we want you to meet. Are you smiling?

See you soon.

Your brother, Frank

LEADERSHIP PRINCIPLE - VISIONARY

One who plans the future with imagination or wisdom.

Abraham Lincoln was a **visionary** when he saw that the nation would one day be reunited again without malice. His death left the door open for radical politicians who wanted to punish the South after the war.

TRULY HISTORIC TRIVIA

- The Lincoln funeral train car was originally his presidential Railroad car, but he never rode in it until his death. It was built by the US Military Railroads and was changed to carry the coffins of both Lincoln and his son, Willie, who died earlier of an illness while Lincoln was living in the White House. The coffins would go from DC and finally end in Illinois.
- As discussed in various parts of this story, Lincoln's stovepipe top hat served as more than fashionable headwear. He used it to store and carry notes, letters, even bills. He called it "His Office."

CHAPTER 5 – WE'VE BEEN RIDING ON THE RAILROAD!
By Harold Scott Smith

I n November of 1867, Willie and I were asked if we'd like to be part of the Pacific Railroad Senatorial Survey Trip from Illinois to Kansas. Within three weeks, we passed through the states of Illinois, Iowa, Nebraska, and Kansas.

By the way, Nebraska had just become a state on March 1st. And at the end of that same month, the United States bought Alaska from Tsar Alexander of Russia for $7.2 million! Somebody said that figured to be two pennies an acre. So how many acres do you think Alaska has?

Buying Alaska was the idea of Secretary of State William H. Seward. People made fun of the purchase and thought that Alaska wasn't worth a hill of beans. It was just mountains, snow and ice. So the newspapers nicknamed the territory "Seward's Folly."

Courtesy of the Library of Congress

Since my oldest brother Frank lived in Kansas, Willie and I decided to get off the train there. He had a candy store (he sold licorice!?) and asked us to come and work for him as we recovered from our military days.

As we traveled, we tried to catch up on the latest news. The newspapers all had stories about adding "Amendments" to our Constitution. The 13th was added to our Constitution in 1865 to protect and provide for the rights or freedoms of African-Americans wherever they lived. (Editor's Note: To amend means to change for the better.)

The Federal Government created the Freedman's Bureau to aid or assist freed slaves, or Freedmen, during the years of reconstruction. After the Civil War, many freed slaves headed north or even out west in order to begin their new lives. The

Bureau provided food, housing, education, healthcare and jobs to our newest citizens. Thus began the journey toward the truths written in the Declaration of Independence so long ago which stated that "All men are created equal."

LEADERSHIP PRINCIPLE - ADVISOR

One who gives his/her opinion on the best plan of action, based on wisdom, intelligence and/or experience.

William H. Seward was a wise **advisor** when he convinced the United States Government to purchase Alaska. It should be no surprise that he was smart enough to see Alaska's potential. He entered college at the age of 15 and believed in a good education for everyone.

TRULY HISTORIC TRIVIA

- Did you know that President Andrew Jackson was the first President to ride on a train?
- Some Train Terminology:

  * A "pearl diver" is a DISHWASHER!

  * A Lamb's Tongue: A fifty cent tip!

CHAPTER 6 – BUFFALOES, INDIANS AND GOLD, OH MY!
By Harold Scott Smith

L ots of changes took place in my life after arriving in Kansas. My big brother Frank and his wife introduced me to a really sweet girl named Kathleen Livingston at their Church. We spent time together going to the barn dances and rodeos.

We were so much alike that it wasn't long before we decided to spend our lives together. (Editor's Note: Though most people today do not get married at 17, many people did in Harry's day.) So, we got married at Anniston Road Baptist Church and settled into a little soddy house that my buddy Willie helped me build. (Editor's Note: Houses on the prairies were built of sod grass.) After a year of working in Frank's store, Willie and I were able to get jobs with the Southern Pacific as Conductors on one of them trains!

Railroads have really changed our lives. We can now get across an entire state in one day! It took a week by stagecoach and a month by foot. Before long, mail order businesses started sending goods by train to our small town from all over our expanding country. My wife Kathleen could buy whatever she wanted or could afford and pick it up at our nearby general store.

Letter from Harold Scott Smith to his wife Kathleen

April 30, 1869

Dear Kathleen,

We have seen thousands of buffalo during our travels through the new western territories. The Cheyenne and Arapahoe hunt them for food and use the hides for clothing and even teepees.

Courtesy of the Library of Congress

They even use their BONES to make tools! YIKES! (Editor's Note: The Cheyenne and Arapahoe were tribes of Native-Americans forced onto the same reservation together in the late 1860s.)

The Indians are nomads. They move their teepee villages as they follow the buffalo herds. But the federal government is trying to relocate the Indians to fixed villages called reservations. The Indians feel that they should not be moved from their native lands and have attacked white settlers. Some soldiers who fought in the Civil War are now trying to keep peace in these territories. They live in Army outposts far from other settlers. The federal government had to create policies, or rules, to protect the settlers and the Indians as tribes continue to be moved into the new reservations.

I'm out here working hard for the Union and Pacific Railroad Companies trying to lay the railroad tracks that will connect with each other and allow us to travel back and forth from the Atlantic Ocean to the Pacific Ocean, connecting the East to the West. I miss you.

Your loving husband,

Harry

Courtesy of the Library of Congress

Here is a picture of Willie and me as we are about to get off the train to be in the picture at Promontory Point, Utah on May 10, 1869. (We are on the left near the smoke stack!) There are railroad officials, political leaders and work gangs gathered at Promontory Point, to drive in the last spike (Editor's Note: like a large nail) connecting the Central Pacific with the Union Pacific line, completing the transcontinental railroad. After the celebration, we hopped on the train to California, where the Gold Rush took place in 1849. People risked their life savings looking for "gold nuggets," but few became wealthy.

A letter from Harold Scott Smith to his parents

January 1869

Dear Ma and Pa,

By the time you read this letter your granddaughter will be six months old. We named her Nancy Jean after your great-great-grandmother. She has blonde hair that seems to bring out the sparkle in her beautiful piercing blue eyes. Like her mother, she seems to be happy all the time. We'd like to have lots of children.

You remember my good buddy, Willie Johnston? He and I are now conductors on the train traveling back and forth between Kansas and the western territories. Our country is growing quickly. Thanks to trains a person can go from coast to coast in 7 days or less. We're meeting so many interesting people. Just yesterday, Dr. Mary Walker was taking the train to a meeting she had back east. She was a surgeon during the Civil War and received the Medal of Honor for her service. (Editor's Note: The Medal of Honor is our country's highest military medal.) Since the war, she's written books and is working to get women the vote.

We are about to stop at our next train station so I'll sign off.

Your son,

Harry

LEADERSHIP PRINCIPLE - EDUCATOR

One who teaches and facilitates learning of new facts, skills, or ideas.

Dr. Mary Walker was an **educator** when she gave lectures on the fact that the U.S. Constitution already gave all people the right to vote. She said that an amendment should not even be necessary to give women rights the Constitution already gave them. Eventually, the 19th Amendment was necessary to outlaw voter discrimination. It was ratified in 1920.

TRULY HISTORIC TRIVIA

- Did you know that the first steam locomotive to establish a regular schedule for passenger service was the 'Best Friend of Charleston'? It made its first trip on Christmas Day, 1830.
- Did you know that, after sleeping in a train seat during a trip, George Pullman designed and built the first sleeping car with fold-out beds in 1862?
- Did you know that from 1865 to 1914 the nation's railway network grew from covering 35,000 to 254,000 miles?

CHAPTER 7 – A MELTING POT OF PEOPLE
By Harold Scott Smith

W illie and I saw some amazing changes in America after our days as drummer boys. The Industrial Revolution changed our whole way of living. As you have read, I grew up on a farm in South Carolina without most of the luxuries we enjoy today. You could probably not imagine living without a phone, but my generation was 26 years old before the first phone rang!

Many inventions were actually a direct result of the mixture of people who moved to our country as immigrants. America is often called the "melting pot" because of the many cultures that make up our land. We owe a lot to immigrants who left their homeland and brought not only their families here but their creative ideas, too. They sought the 'American Dream,' just as we do. Let's take a step back and look at some of the early immigrants.

Chinese immigrants were among those who worked for as little as $28 a month in the 1860s helping to lay the early railroad tracks. They helped build a railroad system with more miles of rails than the total of the rest of the world. Even though they were not always treated fairly, they worked tirelessly to provide for their families.

The country of <u>Scotland</u> gave us Alexander Graham Bell. Have you ever heard of the old saying, "Necessity is the mother of invention?" Bell loved studying sounds which led to his work with the deaf. While doing some research he discovered he could hear sound over a wire. His greatest success was the birth of the telephone in 1876. Now Mr. Bell's invention has been replaced by a smart phone with games and more!

<u>Russian</u> immigrant, Igor Sikorsky, invented the world's first helicopter. He came to the U.S. in 1919 as a young aeronautics engineer.

On the fun side of inventions, immigrants also helped to set the standard for many food and clothing creations. Here are a few examples:

<u>German</u> immigrants first sold HOT DOGS on the streets of New York from their carts in the 1860s. The bun replaced a need for a plate and made the 'dog' easier to carry and eat.

An <u>African-American/Native-American</u> named George Crum, a chef in Saratoga Springs, New York, created potato chips. He simply kept making his famous French fries thinner and thinner until….POTATO CHIPS were invented! Bet you can't just eat one!

Yet another <u>German</u> immigrant, Levi Strauss, created the blue jeans first sold as "waist overalls" that would become the well-loved jeans worn by so many of your generation.

<u>Letter from Harold Scott Smith to his father</u>

June 2, 1892,

Dear Pa,

Your two grandchildren are growing up fast. Nancy-Jean and William are excited to live near the water. We have all moved to New York, as I've taken a job as an immigration officer on Ellis Island in New York Harbor. More than 70% of all immigrants enter the port in New York. The process takes most immigrants between three and five hours. About 20% have to stay overnight in dormitory rooms until their cases can be cleared. However, they don't mind, since the spaces are much better here than on a ship crossing the ocean for days or weeks.

Give Ma a hug for us.

Your son and family (Harry, Kathleen, Nancy-Jean and William)

Sometimes I think we in America tend to forget how the rest of the world watches what we do. Guess that is one of the reasons parents try to teach us to work hard and always do our best. Seems kind of strange that, today in America, we are once again trying to figure out if we want to open our borders, or close them, to those who want to work for their American Dream?!

Courtesy of the Library of Congress

LEADERSHIP PRINCIPLE - INNOVATOR

One who introduces new methods, ideas or products.

Alexander Graham Bell, George Crum and Levi Strauss were all **innovators**. Each inventor made a lasting impression on American technology and culture through his creativity.

TRULY HISTORIC TRIVIA

- Did you know Ellis Island was officially opened in 1892 under President Benjamin Harrison whose grandfather was William Henry Harrison the 9th President?
- Did you know Millions of immigrants came to America from Ireland due to a lack of POTATOES?
- Did you know from inside the main building on Ellis Island one can see the Statue of Liberty which was a gift to us from France in 1886?

New-York Tribune.

PART 6.   SUNDAY, DECEMBER 16, 1906.   EIGHT PAGES.

PRESIDENT ROOSEVELT GATHERING INFORMATION AT FIRST HAND ABOUT THE PANAMA CANAL.

From memoranda dictated on the spot he prepared the message which he will send to Congress to-morrow.

VIEW OF TIVOLI HOTEL FROM ANCON HILL, SHOWING RESERVOIR AND FOUNTAIN. HERE MR. AND MRS. ROOSEVELT WERE GUESTS WHILE ON THE ISTHMUS.

PRESIDENT AND PARTY ON THE LITTLE RAILWAY FROM MOUNT HOPE TO THE RESERVOIR WHICH SUPPLIES COLON.

PRESIDENT ROOSEVELT AND PARTY ON THE VERANDA OF THE STEVENS HOUSE AT CULEBRA.

MR. ROOSEVELT DICTATING MEMORANDA TO SECRETARY ON REAR PLATFORM OF TRAIN.

Courtesy of the Library of Congress

CHAPTER 8 – SPEAK SOFTLY & BUILD A BIG DITCH!
By Harold Scott Smith

R emember our 26th president, Theodore Roosevelt? Well Willie and I met him on Ellis Island as he returned with his son, Kermit from Europe. He asked us to join him on a new adventure – building the Panama Canal!

The Panama Canal was built by the US Army Corps of Engineers. A canal through the country of Panama cut 13,000 nautical miles into 5,200, creating a faster way to ship goods from the Atlantic to the Pacific Ocean.

A second reason for building the canal was to send military ships between the two oceans. This made the Navy better able to move troops and defend our country in times of war. It also helped expand the U.S. by making it easier to get to more territories.

It took the United States ten years to complete the canal. There were many challenges. Diseases, like malaria and yellow fever, spread through the camps of workers. There were also many landslides. Look carefully to the left of the photograph below and you can see Willie and me viewing the 'Big Ditch,' as the Panama Canal was nicknamed.

Roosevelt on a steam shovel at the Panama Canal
Courtesy of the Library of Congress

As the dirt was dug up, we put it on a set of train flat cars. In fact, we were told there was so much dirt being removed it could circle the world four times! The locks of the Panama Canal are seven feet thick...whoa! (Editor's Note: A lock is like a system of gates that raise the ships, like a water elevator, to the level of the canal so they can go through.

Letter from Harold Scott Smith to his wife

October 6, 1907

Dear Kathleen,

   I have sad news today. We were working on the Culebra Cut on the morning of the 4th. As steam shovels broke through and cement was being poured, the mud began shifting and the land came down on us. Willie and I were together as the earth caved in. Sad to say my best buddy did not make it. I'm not exactly sure who got me out of the hole as all of a sudden everything went dark. The next thing I remember is asking where my friend was. William Johnston, drummer boy, Medal of Honor Recipient and my best buddy for over 50 years is gone.

Love,

Harry

(Editor's Note: Official records are not available on how or where the real Willie Johnston died.)

LEADERSHIP PRINCIPLE - VISIONARY

One who plans the future with imagination or wisdom.

Theodore Roosevelt was a **visionary** when he took over the construction of the Panama Canal after the French government abandoned the work. In the 1920s, the canal handled 5,000 ships a year.

TRULY HISTORIC TRIVIA

- Did you know Roosevelt was the first president to travel outside of the continental United States while in office? In 1906, he traveled to Panama.
- Did you know on October 11, 1910, Roosevelt took a four minute flight in a plane built by the Wright brothers, making him the first president to fly in an airplane.

CHAPTER 9 – THE YANKS ARE COMING!
By Harold Scott Smith

I remember the day I heard the terrible news about the sinking of the British ship, *Lusitania*. It was sailing from New York with passengers, even some Americans, and was sunk by the Germans without warning! Our country really did not want to enter a war with Germany, but we could not just sit by and do nothing as they attacked ships at sea.

On April 2, 1917 President Wilson called a meeting with our elected leaders in Congress, and on April 6, 1917 a state of war was declared between our country and Germany. Most of us felt this was a war to make the world safe for democracy – 'the war to end all wars.'

Because of the need for troops, Congress passed a selective draft law which declared that all males between the ages of 18 and 45 could volunteer or be drafted to serve in the US Military.

Two million men in the American Expeditionary Force went to France. Many soldiers were trained at places like Camp Wadsworth (Spartanburg, SC), Camp Jackson (Columbia, SC) and Fort Moultrie (Sullivan's Island, SC) before going to Europe. My grandson Andrew was a marine and went through Parris Island (Port Royal, SC).

Camp Sevier, Greenville (1918)
Courtesy of the U.S. Army

1,261 combat veterans and their commander, General Pershing, were awarded the Distinguished Service Cross, the nation's second highest award for extraordinary heroism. 69 American civilians also received the award. 120 World War I soldiers (8 from South Carolina) received the Medal of Honor. One third of our American men who went to war were either killed or wounded.

Germany agreed to peace on November 11, 1918, and the 'war to end all wars,' was finally over. We had a huge parade in New York with over 10,000 people cheering, whistles tooting, sirens and church bells ringing. We won the war, and believed the world would be a better place on Armistice Day! (Editor's Note: Armistice is a peace treaty between countries.)

Letter from Harold Scott Smith to his daughter

August 1919

Dear Nancy-Jean,

Your nephew, Andrew, just returned from France where he was part of our 'Yanks' serving to keep democracy for all. He looks a bit worn but excited to have been part of restoring peace to the world. Andrew shared with us the new inventions (such as machine guns and tanks) that helped during the battles. The hand grenade was greatly improved and aided in attacking the enemies as they hid in trenches. He said dogs were sometimes used, but troops were apt to adopt them and become too attached.

Was reading in the New York Times that our country's population is over 38 million now! America continues to be the 'melting pot'. There is an article in here about an Irish immigrant named Andrew Carnegie and his steel mill monies being used to build libraries – 3,000 or more. WOW, that's a lot of books!

Much love,

Ma and Pa

LEADERSHIP PRINCIPLE - FACILITATOR

One who makes an action or process easier.

Andrew Carnegie was a **facilitator** when he donated libraries to rural communities like Gaffney, SC. He made it easier for people to have access to books, facilitating their learning.

TRULY HISTORIC TRIVIA

- Did you know that South Carolina received part of Carnegie's money to build the Charleston Library Society, which still serves readers today?
- Did you know that one of the huge heavy-artillery guns that fired the final shots on Nov. 11, 1918 signaling the end of WWI was nicknamed 'Calamity Jane?!'
- Did you know that, for the first time, women served officially in the armed services, though without rank?

CHAPTER 10 - PRESSING THROUGH
THE GREAT DEPRESSION
By Harold Scott Smith

S ometimes it is hard to believe how fast things change in one's life. When I was a kid, we drove horse and buggies or walked almost everywhere. Now many Americans drive automobiles. A fella named Henry Ford came up with the idea of the assembly line to build them faster and cheaper. Before the war, cars were a luxury. Then by the 1920s, mass production became common. In fact, in 1918, 300,000 vehicles were registered. With the affordability of the automobile came the need for highways, motels, service stations, car dealerships and more...BEEP, BEEP!

About the time we were getting used to all the prosperity, the Great Depression hit with a bang! So, what caused this to happen? There was no single cause, but many events worked together to make it happen. A weak banking system, overproduction of goods, over-spending and a bursting credit bubble were some of the reasons.

The Crash of 1929 was one of the main causes of the Great Depression. This stock market crash was the most devastating drop in stock prices in US history. (Editor's Note: A stock is a very small share of ownership in a company. People make money by buying stocks at a low price and selling them when they become popular and prices go up.)

On October 29, 1929, which was called 'Black Tuesday,' the stock market lost $14 billion, making the loss for that week an astounding $30 billion. As news of the crash spread, customers rushed to their banks to withdraw their money. People who had been wealthy lost everything, and many businesses closed. At the peak of the depression, 1 out of 4 people were without work. Rationing, or limited food, caused many Americans to wait in long lines called 'soup lines.' Instead of three meals, some were happy just to get one or two a day. Many children had to quit school to work and help pay for food.

When Franklin D. Roosevelt (FDR) became president, he made a lot of changes to get the country back on its feet. He called these changes a New Deal for America. In South Carolina, my nephew Douglas worked for the Civilian Conservation Corps, one of the organizations created to give people work. The CCC planted trees and built roads. My nephew helped build South Carolina's first state park in Myrtle Beach.

Letter from Harold Scott Smith to his granddaughter, Lorrie

June 29, 1932

Dear Lorrie,

Am enclosing a small scarf your grandma knitted. She asked that I give you this special handiwork. It was her favorite to wear on the 4th of July. Now you can continue the family tradition.

Some say the Depression is about over, but time will tell. I'm grateful that, though it has been difficult, our family has been blessed. Many families were not as fortunate, having to rely on charity like boots from the Boot Fund. Some children live in old boxcars with little comforts like a warm blanket or food. We may not always have second helpings, but at least we don't go to bed hungry. On the bright side, sometimes creativity comes when least expected. I heard that the maker of the Popsicle (called Epicycle at first) has come up with the TWIN Popsicle so it could be shared! Grandma and I love red best.

Much love,

Grandpa and Grandma

LEADERSHIP PRINCIPLE - INNOVATOR

One who introduces new methods, ideas or products.

President Franklin D. Roosevelt was an **innovator** when he came up with a plan to provide jobs while improving infrastructure and the economy. His 'alphabet agencies' (CCC, WPA, CWA) gave people jobs and job training, so they had new hope for the future.

TRULY HISTORIC TRIVIA

- Did you know that during the Great Depression, many children wrote to President and Mrs. Franklin Roosevelt for help? Below are a few examples.
    1. An 18 year old girl asked Mrs. Roosevelt for clothing stored in the White House attic.
    2. A 12 year old girl asked the President and Mrs. Roosevelt for $8.00 for a winter coat.
    3. A child in Kansas asked for help to send his brother to the hospital.
    4. A 13 year old girl sent a Sears & Roebuck order for clothes to Mrs. Roosevelt.

CHAPTER 11- FRANKLIN AND 'THE FIGHTING LADY'
By William Franklin Smith

During World War II, I joined the Navy shortly after the Japanese surprise attack on Pearl Harbor. At the time of the attack, December 7th, 1941, the United States Navy had only 4 aircraft carriers in the Pacific. Fortunately, none of the aircraft carriers were at Pearl Harbor on the day of the surprise attack. If they had been sunk or destroyed that day, the United Sates may not have won the war against the Japanese.

Courtesy of the Naval Historical Center

Within a week after the attack, the United States joined forces with England and her allies in the war against Germany, Italy, and the Japanese. It was now truly a World War. Everyone was signing up to serve, even my 90 year old great-grandpa, Harry, did his part! Due to his age, he knew he wouldn't be part of a fighting group. However, his experience with the railroads and the Panama Canal was special. So, the Seabees made an exception, and allowed him to join them for a short while as a special advisor. (I don't think they knew just how old he was. There were no mandatory birth certificates so it was easy for him to just pick his age!?)

In March, 1943 I was transferred and made a helmsman on the Aircraft Carrier USS Yorktown (CV-10). The job of the helmsman is to steer the 900 foot floating city. (A little more challenging than driving a car!)

Our ship was rushed to completion in only 16 months, which is truly amazing. Most aircraft carriers today take 3-5 years to build. Another interesting fact is that some reports say that up to 75% of the workers that built our ship were women. We called them Rosie the Riveter back then.

Due to the need to hide secrets from the enemy during times of war, there were many mysteries involving the naming of our ship. Names of Navy ships first start with the type of vessel. As an example, CV stands for Carrier Vessel. The '10' represents that the Yorktown was the 10th aircraft vessel to be part of the United

States Navy. It was also tradition to name a ship after a famous military battle, war hero or politician.

The Yorktown (CV- 10) was supposed to be named the Bonhomme Richard after a Revolutionary War battleship captained by a great naval hero, John Paul Jones. But while it was being built at the shipyard in Virginia, the USS Yorktown (CV-5) was sunk by a Japanese submarine during the Battle of Midway in June 1942. A US destroyer sunk the Japanese submarine before it could radio the Japanese Navy of the sinking. The US Navy did not want the Japanese to know that they had sunk one of our carriers. To hide the fact, our carrier was renamed the Yorktown.

During our first year on the Yorktown (CV-10) the US Navy made a documentary/propaganda movie to boost the spirits of the American people at home about our successes in the war. The navy disguised our name by calling us the 'Fighting Lady.' You might catch glimpses of me in that Oscar-winning film!

Our Captain was Joseph J. Clark, the first Native-American to graduate from the United States Naval Academy and command a United States aircraft carrier. Captain Clark was a tough sailor, but he had a funny side to him. Sometimes he would yell orders to our crew, wearing a full Comanche Indian head gear. He also allowed the ship's crew to adopt a dog. The dog had been snuck on board at Pearl Harbor, Hawaii, when we stopped to pick up the planes we were supporting. The dog's name was Scrappy. The pilots loved taking pictures of him in their planes, as if he was the pilot.

In April 1943, we left Virginia and headed to the Pacific Ocean. We went through the same Panama Canal that my great-grandpa and his good buddy Willie helped to build. (I took pictures to send back to him.) From there, we began a month of military exercises in the Hawaiian Islands and headed for our first combat of the war near Marcus Island.

In another battle we joined our sister aircraft carriers, the USS Lexington (CV-16) and USS Cowpens (CV-L 25). The Cowpens was named after the Revolutionary War battle that American's won against the British in South Carolina. During battle, our aviators were quick to give protection to our troops on the ground as they fought the Japanese.

One day, during the Marshall campaign, I was standing my watch in the wheel house steering the ship. We were at battle stations, everyone was awake either assisting in the take-off and landing of planes or manning a gun or fire station. Suddenly, all the men on the flight deck were pointing upward where we saw a lone plane high in the sky. It was not one of ours, as our planes would leave or return on specific course directions that only the ship's crew and pilots knew. Suddenly, the plane started diving straight at us in an apparent suicide dive. Our anti-aircraft guns scored numerous hits; however, what was left of the plane grazed the side of our ship, and exploded as it hit the water. The explosion broke my coffee cup as I was holding it!

Our greatest success was the day our pilots discovered the Japanese battleship Yamato in 1945. The Yamato was the largest ship in the Japanese Navy. But she was no match for our pilots. It was a great day as planes from all of our carriers in Air Group 9 watched her explode and sink. We knew that we were winning the war.

However, the proudest day of my military career was a month later when we picked up a group of Seabees from the Island of Guam. Great-grandpa Harold Smith had been advising a Seabee unit that was supporting the Army and Marines by building roads and bridges. Due to the limited information that was allowed to be disclosed in letters home, he had no idea that I was serving on the USS Yorktown when he stepped on board in 1945. I have to say, we cried tears of joy when we met on the flight deck.

It was during the next month as we steamed home to San Francisco, that he told me the stories about his time in the Pacific.

LEADERSHIP PRINCIPLE – EDUCATOR

One who teaches and facilitates learning of new facts, skills, or ideas.

Captain Joseph J. Clark was not only the captain of a ship, he was also an **educator**. When the United States entered World War II, there was little time to properly train sailors. They had to learn through on-the-job training from their more experienced superior officers, like Captain Clark.

TRULY HISTORIC TRIVIA

- Did you know that during WWII, Navy ships were 'Island Hopping' across the Pacific? It is sort of like 'leap frog'. We were taking over islands from the Japanese, one by one, until we reached our ultimate goal - JAPAN!
- Did you know that chocolate cookies were made 10,000 at a time in the ship's bakery? With 3,300 men on the ship, how many cookies do you think each man would get?
- The Hangar Deck, the main deck where the planes are stored and worked on below the flight deck, is 40,000 square feet, the same size of Bill Gates', founder of Microsoft, home.

CHAPTER 12 - SEABEES, "WE BUILD, WE FIGHT!"
By Harold Scott Smith

After the Japanese surprise attack on Pearl Harbor, and the United States entering the war on the European continent, I remember that everyone was walking around in a daze. How could this happen? We were one of the greatest countries on earth. If the Japanese could attack Hawaii, what was stopping them from attacking San Francisco or Charleston? Once again, we were preparing for war.

My grandson, Andrew, wanted to serve. But, the army would not let him enlist due to the injuries he received in WWI. Instead, he worked as a civilian on designing better equipment for the servicemen. He knew that what he was doing was important to help his son (and my great-grandson), William, stay safe and win the war.

And then there was me, a great-great-grandpa. Can you believe it? Because of my experience building the Panama Canal, the government let me go with the Seabees as a consultant. The

Seabees was a construction unit formed by the Navy shortly after the attack on Pearl Harbor. More than 325,000 men served with the Seabees in World War II, fighting and building on six continents and more than 300 islands. In the Pacific, where most of the construction work was needed, the Seabees landed soon after the Marines and built airstrips, bridges, roads, gasoline storage tanks, and huts for warehouses, hospitals, and housing.

I helped design over 100 bridges and dams during the war. There was one bridge the Seabees built 10 times. Once it was completed, the Japanese would find a way to blow it up.

Here is a letter I wrote to my daughter, Nancy-Jean, after I made my decision to join up.

Letter from Harold Scott Smith to his daughter, Nancy-Jean Smith

December 20, 1941

Dear Nancy-Jean,

Please do not try to talk me out of my decision, as it is something I must do. By the time you read this, I will be on my way on board the USS Hornet as a Seabee to help build roads, bridges and other needed construction projects for our land troops. Even though many of us are too old to be soldiers, our experience in building is needed.

Our first project is top secret, so I cannot share, but our group's slogan is "We Build, We Fight!" We are not raw or young recruits but experienced and skilled. Many of us helped to build the Panama Canal, Boulder Dam, highways and even some New York Skyscrapers, too. Of course, I'm a consultant and won't be using a shovel or a gun. But the younger ones have been trained in military discipline and the use of light firearms. They do not really expect to need them.

My battalion is being sent over immediately to begin building urgent naval sites. One of our main duties will be to handle, assemble, launch and put in place pontoon (like a floating bridge) causeways. Each of us has experience building much of what will be needed, just not in a war.

Before I close, I met a Colonel Jimmy Doolittle, today. He is a pilot who flies B-25 Bombers. They are large but amazing planes. By the time you read this letter, I am sure you are going to hear about Doolittle and his raiders in the newspapers.

With love,

Pa

Our only source of news was what we heard on the radio, read in the paper, or from the weekly newsreels played on downtown's big screen theater. I remember after the war when my daughter,

Nancy-Jean, told me about the night she was listening to the radio and news about Doolittle's successful raid on Japan was broadcast. It was as if the Chicago Cubs had won the World Series. Everyone was jumping and yelling in the street. The next morning, the story was front page in the daily paper.

Seabees recruiting poster
Courtesy of the Library of Congress

LEADERSHIP PRINCIPLE - INNOVATOR

One who introduces new methods, ideas or products.

Colonel James Doolittle was an **innovator** when he came up with the idea of flying B-25 bombers from an aircraft carrier and landing them in China. He was thinking outside the box and pulled off a plan that seemed impossible.

TRULY HISTORIC TRIVIA

- Did you know that during WWII Seabees built over 100 bases using pontoon- like structures called "magic boxes" to help foot soldiers escape?
- Did you know that at one location, the Seabees moved over ONE MILLION cubic yards of dirt and rocks to build a needed road?
- Did you know Seabees even landed with the American troops on Normandy in 1942 and again on D-Day on 6 June 1944?

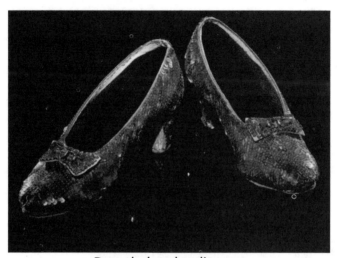
Dorothy's ruby slippers
Courtesy of the Smithsonian
National Museum of American History

CHAPTER 13 - MICKEY MOUSE, MUSIC, MOVIES & MORE!
By Harold Scott Smith

L et's take a break from all the talk of war and go back to some of the fun times. If you remember, I was born in 1850, so I've been witness to lots of fads and inventions. My favorite building opened in the 1930s - the world's tallest building, the Empire State Building. The PB&J sandwich became famous in 1922 and continues to be my favorite!

Who knows - maybe YOU have an idea in that creative mind of yours that could change American culture even more? Here are a few of my favorite things through the decades!

Mickey Mouse - As Walt Disney shares the story "... a fellow kept hanging around my hotel waving $300 at me and saying that he wanted to put the Mouse on the paper tablets children use in school. As usual, Roy and I needed money, so I took the $300." The rest is Mickey Mouse history!

Dance – In the 1920s, people loved to dance, especially the Charleston and the Fox-Trot. Dance marathons were something everyone went to every weekend. (The longest dance marathon ever recorded lasted for 3 weeks.)

Radio – This was a great invention that changed our culture forever. Whole families gathered around the radio every night to listen to music, comedy, dramas, news and live events. We could now hear the news (sometimes as it happened) and not just read about it the next day in the newspaper. During the Depression, President Roosevelt gave 'fireside chats' over the radio to give the American public the latest information on our government and how our economy was doing.

Movies - The movie theater was the latest thing. Believe it or not, the first 3-D movie was in the 1920s. My favorite movies were: Gone with the Wind (1939), Bright Eyes (1934) with Shirley Temple (known for her blonde ringlets and her ability to sing and tap dance), and The Wizard of Oz (1939) with my favorite character, the Scarecrow, and my favorite quote; "I could be another Lincoln if I only had a brain."

Music - The "Star Spangled Banner" became our national anthem in 1931. My favorite singer in the 1940s was Bing Crosby. Most people know him best as the man who sang "White Christmas."

The 1940's was a great decade for fads, too. The Frisbee was invented in 1948 when kids tossed metal pie plates to one another. They were later were made out of plastic. Lots of women liked to sew and some made clothes out of old table cloths! In 1947, Jackie Robinson became the first black man to play Major League Baseball. He won the National League's Most Valuable Player Award two years later. Boxing was another hit in the world of sports. George M. Cohan was an American playwright, songwriter, actor, singer, dancer and producer. He published more than 300 songs during his lifetime, including "Yankee Doodle Boy" and "You're a Grand Old Flag."

Each decade is full of awe-inspiring moments in history. Even in the midst of war, our country tried to find a way to make life better - whether encouraging one another through words, lyrics set to music or even just with smiles. From my days as a drummer boy meeting President Lincoln to my days serving as a Seabee in WWII, my life has been anything but common.

Here is a letter to my newest great-great-grandson, Benjamin Jackson Smith, on the day he was born. He couldn't read it yet, but I knew that someday it would mean a lot. By the way, why don't you stop and write a letter of appreciation to someone? (It doesn't cost much to send a letter. The first stamps in our country cost 3 cents in 1842.)

<u>Letter from Harold Scott Smith to Benjamin Jackson Smith</u>

February 8, 1945

Dear Great-great-grandson,

Welcome to our family as our newest Smith! I'm your great-great-grandpa, and as of this letter I'm 95 years young. I have enclosed our family tree, including YOU, my first great-great-grandson! (see next page)

You have a rich family heritage of service to our country. We have been in every military battle since the Civil War. We have had just about every job created since our arrival to this country through Charleston long ago - farmers, merchants, carpenters, road construction workers, tailors, cobblers (shoe makers) and of course soldiers and sailors.

We live in a wonderful land of freedom and opportunity. Always do your part to keep it free. Though I will probably not be part of your life much longer, I know that your pa will guide you as my pa guided me growing up in South Carolina before the Civil War.

God bless you,

Great-great-grandpa

DESCENDANTS OF

Great-great-grandpa Harold Scott Smith (1850)

Name	Birth Year
Great-grandpa William Andrew Smith	1872
Granpa Andrew Smith	1900
Your pa William Franklin Smith	1925
YOU Benjamin Jackson Smith	1945

LEADERSHIP PRINCIPLE – COMMUNICATOR

One who gets his/her point across effectively.

President Franklin D. Roosevelt was an effective **communicator** when he held his 'fireside chats' each month during the Great Depression. His encouragement and updates on economic progress made him one of America's most popular presidents. Many people even kept a portrait of him in their homes.

TRULY HISTORIC TRIVIA

- Did you know that the 1930s was a most historic decade for movies? 'The Wizard of Oz', 'Gone with the Wind', 'King Kong', and 'Snow White' were in theaters then.
- Did you know that it was Walt Disney's wife Lillian who came up with the name Mickey for the mouse? Walt Disney originally named him Mortimer Mouse!

CHAPTER 14 - "FAREWELL, GREAT-GRANDPA"
By William Franklin Smith

My name is William "Franklin" Smith, great-grandson of Harold Scott Smith. We were all watching the New York Yankees beat the Brooklyn Dodgers on the television last night in his cottage when he fell ill. Dr. Hanna came quickly, but Great-Grandpa's 102 year old heart finally needed a rest. His last words to us were, "Please keep being story tellers and journaling so future generations will know the wonders I've witnessed as an American."

102 years is a long time to live in this country, and Great-Grandpa saw a lot in his lifetime. He was able to see much of our history, from his days as a drummer boy in the Civil War to his days with the Seabees in World War II. My great-grandpa was a man who learned to work on the family farm back before the labor saving tools he saw come to pass. His dad, my great-great-grandpa, taught him at an early age the value of always striving to do one's best, and he lived his life doing so.

It is really hard to say "good-bye," but he would have wanted us to follow his example and continue building an even better America for our family. Tomorrow will be his funeral service with his burial to follow in South Carolina next week. We are taking him home by one of the inventions that not only changed America but changed Great-grandpa, too. Because of his love of trains, he served many years as a conductor. One of his favorite, though sad, train tales was of being part of the Honor Guard assigned to take President Lincoln to his final resting place back in 1865. He often wept as he shared stories of his days with the 16th President of the United States.

He did have one funny story about the time some English visitors came to "Lincoln's Cottage," which was located a few miles from the White House. Mrs. Lincoln had already retired for the evening, but the President came to greet the guests IN HIS NIGHTGOWN! Once they were satisfied with seeing the president, he sent them on their way and went to bed.

Our family's desire will always be to follow in the footsteps of our family hero and mentor, Great-grandpa Harry. He was always positive and encouraging to all who met him. His love of family and friends is something we will all miss. Below is the death notice as it appeared in his favorite newspaper, "The New York Times," He made us promise to use his favorite picture from when he was an old drummer boy.

"July 8, 1952 - Harold Scott Smith, 102, passed away last evening in his cottage with his family by his side. He was well known for his service to his country from the age of 11 until he finally retired in 1945. Though raised in South Carolina, "Harry" joined the Union Army as a drummer boy. He switched to the bugle and became in much demand to play the song "TAPS."

He is survived by his son, William, daughter Nancy Jean, a grandson Andrew, granddaughters Lorrie and Kathleen, a great-grandson, William Franklin and a great-great-grandson Benjamin Jackson. His friends are too numerous to mention, but they were all a blessing in his life. One of his favorite quotes was "Never underestimate the power of an encouraging word," and he truly lived his life as an encourager and friend. His humor and love of God and country are memories we will always hold dear. His final burial will take place in Magnolia Cemetery in Charleston, South Carolina next to his beloved wife."

"Harry" and his best friend Willie
*Courtesy of the collection of Michael Welch
& the Congressional Medal of Honor Society*

LEADERSHIP PRINCIPLE - MOTIVATOR

One who gives others a reason to act or perform a task.

Great-grandpa Harold Scott Smith was a **motivator** who showed his children, grandchildren, and great-grandchildren the value of remembering the past and documenting the present.

TRULY HISTORIC TRIVIA

- Did you know the battle flag of the Pee Dee Light Artillery was never surrendered and is today in the Confederate Relic Room and Military Museum in Columbia, SC?
- Did you know that Stonewall Jackson was the leader of the Pee Dee Light Artillery after the Seven Days Battle? (The same Stonewall Jackson who would lose his arm and life a short while later.)
- Did you know that in the war "Harry" (Great-grandpa) became best friends with Willie Johnston who was the youngest Medal of Honor recipient at 13 years old?

CHAPTER 15 – WHAT IS A COLD WAR?
By William Franklin Smith

H aving been part of World War II, I thought that after the victory we shared with Russia, a friendly bond would have developed between our countries. But Russia's form of government was based on Communism, or the belief that government should control the people. In America, our government is based on Democracy - the belief that government should protect our freedom in 'life, liberty and the pursuit of happiness'. The differences between our countries' core beliefs caused conflicts.

The United Nations was established in 1945 to promote peace between countries. But at the same time, distrust and a 'cold war' grew between Communist and Democratic nations, particularly the United States and Russia (a.k.a. USSR – United Soviet Socialist Republic). During the Cold War, USSR and United States governments spied on each other and competed in an arms race (building and storing nuclear weapons).

The scariest time of the Cold War was the Cuban Missile Crisis. In October, 1962 Americans were glued to their TV sets waiting to see if President John F. Kennedy would succeed in getting the USSR to remove their nuclear missiles from Cuba. It was like a very dangerous game of 'chicken,' and we thought we were on the brink of a nuclear war. Imagine our relief when Kennedy won the stand-off.

Not all rockets were made into nuclear weapons during the Cold War. Some were designed to go into space! In the 1950s, the USSR and the USA got involved in a space race. In 1957, Russia launched two Sputnik rockets into space. One of them carried a dog named Laika into orbit! The following year (1958), our government formed NASA (National Aeronautics & Space Administration).

By the time John F. Kennedy became president, the USSR was getting ahead of us. We had sent the first spy and weather satellites into orbit, but they had already sent unmanned spacecraft around the moon and the sun! Then in April 1961, they sent the first man, Yuri Gagarin, into space (one month before our astronaut, Alan Shepard, got there). So President Kennedy challenged Congress and NASA to be the first to put a man on the moon!

On Christmas Eve, December 24, 1968, the crew of Apollo 8 was the first to orbit the moon. Once again, American's were glued to their TV sets as the first live pictures of the moon were sent from astronauts (Frank Borman, James Lovell, and William Anders). I was still serving my country as a sailor on board the USS Yorktown. In my 20 years on 'the Fighting Lady', I rose to the rank of Chief Petty Officer, the highest rank of an enlisted man. I was on the flight deck on December 27th when we pulled the astronauts and their capsule out of the Pacific. That was how they landed in those days – a splash down in the ocean and a ride home on an aircraft carrier. What a strange feeling it was to shake the hands of men who had just been around the moon, and to touch a capsule that went into space!

Seven months later, in 1969, Neil Armstrong (a former Navy pilot) took 'one small step for man, one giant leap for mankind' when he became the first person to walk on the moon. Once again, Americans got to watch the whole thing from their living rooms.

Television screens were black and white in those days, and the picture wasn't anything as good as HD. I bet you didn't know that Great-grandpa Harry Smith got to watch one of the very first TVs in the 1940s. Here's a letter he wrote telling me about it.

Letter from Harold Smith to William Franklin Smith

June 14, 1947

Dear William Franklin and family,

I have moved to the New York State Soldiers and Sailors Home at Bath, New York. I am grateful to the Woman's Relief Corps that persuaded this state to maintain a home for us Veterans way back in 1890. It's a peaceful location. The food is pretty good, too, but will never compare to your Ma's cooking and those wonderful collards and corn bread with vinegar sauce.

By the way, we are going to be one of six experimental stations for this new invention called a television. They are placing one in the recreation room near the library for all of us guys to watch. We hope to watch sports on it. You know how much I love baseball.

Love you all,

Great-grandpa

Courtesy of the Library of Congress

LEADERSHIP PRINCIPLE - ADVISOR

One who gives his/her opinion on the best plan of action, based on wisdom, intelligence and/or experience.

President Kennedy surrounded himself with **advisors** during the Cuban Missile Crisis. One such advisor was his National Security Advisor McGeorge Bundy who first informed him that Russia was placing nuclear missiles on the island of Cuba. And Kennedy was an advisor, too, when he suggested that NASA be the first to put a man on the moon.

TRULY HISTORIC TRIVIA

- Did you know that no new invention entered American homes faster than black and white television sets? 1 out of 3 homes had one by 1952.
- Did you know that a 16 inch black and white TV Screen, AM/FM radio and 3-speed phonograph in a mahogany veneer cabinet sold for only $339.95. That would be about $3,600 today!
- Did you know that the USSR sent the first woman into space in 1963? Her name was Valentia Tereshkova
- Did you know that the first 'Earthlings' to orbit the moon were two Russian turtles in 1968?

CHAPTER 16 - INTERNMENT IN TIMES OF WAR
By William Franklin Smith

W e have been going through lots of Great-grandpa's journals. He really loved to write down his thoughts. His writings are entertaining and educational at times. Believe it or not, he left a journal for each of the ten decades of his life ...WHOA! He may be gone, but his words and his life live on through us and the stories he shared.

One of Great-grandpa's journals shares stories about a sad time in history known as 'Internment.'   Internment is the act of detaining a person or a group of people, especially a group perceived to be a threat during wartime. The first internment he wrote about was the Holocaust.

The Holocaust was the persecution and murder of approximately six million Jews by Germany's Nazi regime. Did you ever read about Anne Frank? She was one of over one million Jewish children who died in the Holocaust. She was born on June

12, 1929 in Frankfurt, Germany. We know much about her because, like Great-grandpa, she wrote down her thoughts in a diary (which is a type of journal).

Japanese-Americans were another group he wrote about. 62% of those in internment camps were actually American citizens. Following the bombing of Pearl Harbor in 1941, over 110,000 persons were relocated to camps with most of them being school-age children, infants or young adults. He was especially moved by the story of a young teenager named Mary. She was but 16 when she and her family were uprooted and moved to one of many internment camps located inside our US borders. Even while they were imprisoned behind barbed wires, her brother was drafted into the US Army. Today she lives in Baltimore, Maryland with her family and is a productive and loyal citizen.

No one in our family fought in the Korean War, which was a conflict between Communist and non-Communist forces from June 1950 to July 1953. But I had a friend who was a POW (prisoner of war) during that time. According to U.S. officials, 7,245 Americans were held in POW camps during the Korean War. Of these, 2,806 died in captivity, 4,418 were released, and 21 refused freedom and chose voluntarily to go live in the People's Republic of China.

Great-grandpa did not write about Korea. (He was nearly 100 when it started!) But my friend told me about an Army Chaplain named Emil Kapaun who volunteered to be a <u>POW</u> so he could take care of wounded soldiers who were being taken prisoner by the enemy. On the long march to the prison camp, he encouraged the wounded soldiers to keep up (knowing they might die if they didn't) and even carried one who couldn't walk. While in the prison camp, he risked his own life by sneaking out at night to find extra food for the sick and starving prisoners. Just goes to show you – a hero doesn't have to fight as a soldier. A person can be a hero by taking care of others.

Holocaust Memorial at the California Legion of Honor, San Francisco
Courtesy of the Library of Congress

LEADERSHIP PRINCIPLE - MOTIVATOR

One who gives others a reason to act or perform a task.

Chaplain (Captain) Emil J. Kapaun was a **motivator** when he encouraged the prisoners to be strong. He gave them hope during the most trying time of their lives, and they gave him credit after the war for keeping them alive in the POW camp.

TRULY HISTORIC TRIVIA

- Did you know that, although he died while in the POW camp during the Korean War, Chaplain Kapaun finally received the Medal of Honor in 2013? It was given to his closest relative – a nephew.
- Did you know that the most famous POW camp during the Vietnam War was nicknamed the 'Hanoi Hilton' by American prisoners? Hoa Lo Prison was originally for political prisoners and was converted to a POW camp where the North Vietnamese Army interrogated prisoners by torture.

CHAPTER 17 - WOMEN, WEAPONS AND WAR
By Benjamin Jackson Smith

M y great-great-grandpa used to say that we forget women have been involved in every war we've been in from the Revolutionary War through today! So, let me share some of their stories as he would. His stories began with WWII and went all the way back to our country's early days.

Courtesy of the Library of Congress

Women and WWII

Great-great-grandpa used to tell us about 'Rosie the Riveter' and 'Wendy the Welder'. These were nicknames for women who worked in factories as defense workers. Among other things, they built and designed ships and planes! Since millions of men were enlisted or drafted during the war, women filled the gap in the labor force back here at home. All of that while still providing care for their children. Believe it or not, by 1945 nearly 1 of every 4 married women worked outside the home.

Women also served in the military during World War II. Some 350,000 women served in the U.S. Armed Forces, both in the states and abroad. Some women flew the same airplanes that other women built.

Women and WWI

Though public opinion was even more negative toward women working outside the home, 21,480 U.S. Army nurses (military nurses were all women then) served in military hospitals in the United States and overseas during World War I. Eighteen African-American Army nurses served stateside caring for German prisoners of war (POWs) and African-American soldiers. After the war, these women entered the Army Nurse Corps.

The first American women who enlisted into the regular armed forces were 13,000 women admitted into active duty in the Navy and Marines during World War I. A much smaller number were admitted into the Coast Guard. They mostly served in clerical positions (typing, filing papers and answering phones) but did receive the same benefits as men. ($28.75 per month was the average salary!) However, long before any American troops served on foreign soil, American women were already serving 'over there' as volunteers, nurses in transportation and with other war relief agencies. You might recognize some of these groups today. The Salvation Army, Young Men's Christian Association (YMCA) and the American Red Cross.

Women and the Civil War

There were over 400 proven cases of women who fought as soldiers in the Civil War. Many dressed to look like men and fought for the causes they believed in. Other women played important roles as spies. Harriet Tubman, famous for the Underground Railroad, was also a nurse and a spy for the Union army. She blew up a Confederate supply depot.

Harriet Tubman, *Courtesy of the Library of Congress*

There were also many women who served as nurses. Florence Nightingale trained professional nurses to take care of the wounded. It is said that as many as 8,000 women served as nurses during the war, including Louisa May Alcott (author of *Little Women*) who wrote letters home for wounded and dying soldiers. Sally Tompkins was a captain in the Confederate Army and ran a hospital in Richmond, Virginia. She saved countless lives by insisting on cleanliness which prevented infections.

Women and the Revolutionary War

During the American Revolution, Mary Hays (a.k.a. Molly Pitcher) is said to have followed her husband to the Battle of Monmouth. She carried pitchers of water for cooling the cannons and the soldiers, thereby earning her nickname. Supposedly, after her husband collapsed, she took his place at the cannon and served heroically through the battle.

Thousands of women were active in the American Revolution, and most were the wives or daughters of officers or soldiers. They were almost always visible in military camps and were called 'camp followers.' Because women frequently did not serve any military function during the war, their individual names were never listed in the records and are unknown to us today.

Yes, there were women soldiers and spies in this war, too. Deborah Sampson of Massachusetts cut her hair and fought as Robert Shurtliff in New York in 1781. After a year in the army, she was found out and had to go home. 18 year old Emily Geiger from South Carolina was one. Rather than be caught with the note she was to deliver to General Greene, she memorized the message, ate it piece by piece and was released. The next day she delivered the message verbally!

LEADERSHIP PRINCIPLE - FACILITATOR

One who makes an action or process easier.

Harriett Tubman was a **facilitator** as both a conductor on the Underground Railroad and as a spy for the Union Army. She risked her own life to make it easier for slaves to find freedom and to help the Union Army.

TRULY HISTORIC TRIVIA

- Did you know that Andrew Jackson's mother Elizabeth Hutchinson Jackson died trying to nurse others to health in the Lowcountry during the Revolutionary War and is buried in Charleston?
- Did you know that as of 2012, the total number of active women in the military was 204,973?
- Did you know the WWI "Hello Girls" (pictured previous page) were a group of US Army telephone operators who were trained by AT&T?

CHAPTER 18 – WOMEN AT WORK
By William Franklin Smith

W illiam "Franklin" here, again, sharing memories from Great-grandpa's day and beyond about the ever changing role of women in society. It was during the Industrial Revolution (late 18th and early 19th centuries) that hundreds of women began working outside the home in factories. Great-grandpa loved to share his father's stories about this time in America.

<u>Women and Social Change</u>

Great-grandpa often spoke about Abolitionists (people who wanted to end slavery). Lucretia Mott and Elizabeth Cady Stanton were two women who had the courage to speak out against slavery. During their time, almost everyone believed women should not have an active role in politics. Great-grandpa always said it was important that an individual make the world a better place in word and deed.

Before the Civil War, many women were involved in groups called Benevolent Societies. These groups worked to help those less fortunate such as orphans and the poor. Women's suffrage (the right to vote) groups also became increasingly influential. Great-grandpa always said 'women were able to thread their influence throughout history, even before they gained the right to vote in America in 1920!'

African-American women were a powerful force for social change even before the Civil Rights Movement. Mary McLeod Bethune from Sumter County, SC (whose parents had been slaves before the Civil War) became Special Advisor on Minority Affairs to President Franklin D. Roosevelt. And let's not forget the 'Queen Mother of the Civil Rights Movement' Septima Clark (also from South Carolina). She helped found Citizenship Schools throughout the south to teach African-Americans how to read – a requirement to vote during the Jim Crow Era. When Dr. Martin Luther King received the Nobel Peace Prize, he invited Septima Clark to go with him because of her contribution.

Women on the Job

Today, there is no job women can't do. Women have made and continue to make outstanding contributions. Education was one career field that provided great opportunities for women. In the 1860s, several new state universities began to allow both women and men to attend (co-education). Mary Gordon Ellis graduated from Winthrop College in 1913. She was the Superintendent of Education in Jasper County in the 1920s and became the first woman elected to the South Carolina State Senate in 1928.

Women have made contributions in other fields as well.

* Bennettsville native Marian Wright Edelman became the first African-American female attorney in Mississippi in 1964.

* Dr. Elizabeth Blackwell was the first American female physician.

* Maria Mitchell was the first American female Astronomer.

* Madam Marie Curie and her husband announced the discovery of radium and won the Nobel Prize twice!

Women in Space

Dr. Sally Ride in space, *Courtesy of NASA*

The First American Woman in Space was Sally Ride who, in 1983, boarded the space shuttle *Challenger,* where she played a vital role in helping deploy communications satellites. She also became the first American woman to travel to space a second time. On that flight she used the shuttle's robotic arm to remove ice from the shuttle's exterior and readjust a radar antenna. In 2013, she received the Presidential Medal of Freedom (posthumously - she died in 2012).

Christa McAuliffe, *Courtesy of NASA*

In 1986, the first teacher astronaut, Christa McAuliffe, boarded the *Challenger* space shuttle as the first citizen to travel toward the heavens. Sadly the *Challenger* and all 7 aboard did not survive that mission due partly to the wind shear on that chilly Florida morning. Thousands watched, including McAuliffe's family and students back home via television. "Teacher in Space" Christa

McAuliffe taught high school social studies in New Hampshire. Here is a quote from her journal, "*just as the pioneer travelers of the Conestoga wagon days kept personal journals, I as a space traveler would do the same.*"

From the pilgrims to the pilots of today, women have always played a key role in our country. Who knows where women will travel next?! Here is a letter written to my granddaughter, Anne Hutchinson Smith on her 18th birthday.

<u>Letter from William Franklin Smith to Anne Hutchinson Smith</u>

June 2, 1988

Dear Granddaughter,

Happy 18th Birthday, Anne! As your granddad, I was just going through some of your great-great-great-grandpa's journals (Harry), on his 102 years of life in America. He would be very proud of the young lady you have become. You will be the FIRST SMITH FEMALE in the Navy! Yes, I will be there standing proud next month as you join the US Navy.

Love,

Granddad

LEADERSHIP PRINCIPLE - EDUCATOR

One who teaches and facilitates learning of new facts, skills, or ideas.

Septima Clark was an **educator** who taught people how to read, so they could exercise their rights as free citizens in a democracy. In doing that, she also benefitted them in countless ways. Reading is a fundamental skill we all need.

TRULY HISTORIC TRIVIA

- Did you know that 7.5 million people were employed by women-owned businesses in 2007?
- Did you know that the wrestler (male or female) who held the title of World Champion longest (1956 – 1987) was 'The Fabulous Moolah' Lillian Ellison from South Carolina?
- Did you know that the first European born in America was a girl named Virginia Dare?
- Did you know who wrote this in her diary? "Parents can only give good advice or put them on the right paths, but the final forming of a person's character lies in their own hands."(Anne Frank's diary entry for July 15, 1944)

CHAPTER 19 – 'I' IS FOR INVENTIONS & IPADS, TOO!
By William Franklin Smith

As we have been going through more of Great-grandpa's journals, it is unbelievable all the inventions created in his lifetime. My son Benjamin and I even discovered a wooden box under his bed full of old newspaper articles from President Lincoln's death in 1865 until right before his own death in 1952.

You probably remember that an invention is a creative thought or idea; a new object, device or process that no one has seen or heard of before. To keep someone's ideas from being taken, an inventor will get a patent, which means that only the inventor can make money from his invention. A copyright works the same way for writers of books. (You should be writing down your ideas!) Did you know that the only US President to hold a patent (so far) was Abraham Lincoln? And the first African-American to hold a patent was Thomas L. Jennings, a free man and business owner in New York? He invented a method of dry cleaning clothes in 1821.

Telegraphs & Telephones

Communication is a word for sharing of information. In Great-grandpa's day writing letters was the most popular way to communicate. Then the telegraph, telephone, radio and television were all invented during his lifetime. He used to say that they were all one big invention.

Samuel Morse invented the electric telegraph in 1836 (building on the prior work of others, of course). Morse developed and shared with our US Congress his invention, successfully sending the first message, "What hath God wrought?" Oh, if you are ever visiting our US Capitol in DC there is a bronze marker located on the exact spot!

Whoa….did you hear that ringing? Just think; if you lived before 1876 you never would have had to answer the phone. But then, of course, no one knew what a phone was until Alexander Graham Bell invented it. The telephone actually transmitted a person's voice over copper wires, instead of just beeps that spelled out the Morse code. Of all the early inventions, this one continues to enhance our lives daily.

Thomas Alva Edison's many inventions changed the world, also. The one he's most known for is his work with the incandescent light bulb. You might say he lit up our world. Funny, but one of

Edison's first jobs was as a telegraph operator working Morse's invention. Altogether, Edison patented 1,093 inventions. He often said, "Genius is one percent inspiration and 99 percent perspiration." (By the way, the first underarm deodorant was called Mum and was invented by a mystery inventor in 1888. Glad Edison knew that, too!) Edison died in 1931, and Great-grandpa kept the article about all the electric lights in the United States being dimmed for one minute as a tribute to his life.

All these changes in communication and technology have made our world seem smaller in some ways. In Great-grandpa's 102 years, he went from a world where it might take weeks to hear news from across our country to watching the events occurring on the other side of the globe as they happened. He even got pretty good using the telephone. Sometimes he would let it ring just for the 'noise,' as he often called it.

That Does Not Compute?!

In the 1940s and 1950s, one computer filled an entire room and weighed about 30 tons! (An anchor on the USS Yorktown weighs half that! Imagine moving that computer to your room.) As technology continued to develop, computers have gotten smaller.

Believe it or not, mechanical computing devices were in existence in the 1800s. There were even rare devices that could be considered computers in ancient times, but electronic computers were invented in the 20th century.

A computer takes information in, and is able to manipulate or process it into a useful format. Then it outputs the information for us to use as needed. When controlled by skilled programmers, computers can accomplish amazing feats. Some high-performance military aircraft wouldn't be able to fly without constant computerized adjustments to flight control. Computers help us put spacecraft into orbit, control medical testing equipment, and create films and video games.

All of us rely on computers every day in one way or another. In fact, the writing of this book relied heavily on my office computer and the one in my head ...as in my brain! Computers let us store large chunks of information and find a specific piece of it almost instantly. Many of the things we take for granted in the world wouldn't work without computers - from cars to power plants to cell phones.

Great-grandpa never imagined being able to Skype with friends and family globally. (Actually, that still does not compute with me either.) In 1969, the Military began working with something called the 'Internet'. It was a special project which, as we can all agree, worked out well.

Google It

Believe it or not, Google began as a research project! Sure hope they got an A+. Google, Inc. was officially formed on September 4, 1998 in a garage in Menlo Park, California. (Not sure where the cars were!)

An Apple for an iPad?

The story of Apple's iPad began in 2010. It is incredible; especially considering it is only 3 years old. Like most inventions, it was built upon decades of ideas, tests, products and more ideas. Today an iPad can shoot video, take photos, play music, and perform internet functions such as web-browsing and emailing. Other functions (games, reference, GPS navigation, social networking, etc.) can be enabled by downloading and installing apps (software applications). As of 2013, the App Store offered more than 900,000 apps!

Before we close this chapter, let's email my granddaughter, Anne. She is serving as a Pilot on the USS Lincoln. The USS Lincoln is one of the first nuclear powered aircraft carriers to allow women aboard!

Email from William Franklin Smith to Anne Hutchinson Smith

February 12, 2013   8:15 pm

Dear Anne,

Today is your ship's namesake's birthday... as in Abraham Lincoln. We heard that the U.S. Department of Defense announced that the ship's scheduled overhaul (repair work) will be delayed due to lack of money in the budget. Guess that will give y'all a bit more time to train and relax perhaps? Please be safe out there. Will email again soon.

Love,

Granddad,

LEADERSHIP PRINCIPLE - INNOVATOR

One who introduces new methods, ideas or products.

All **innovators** of new technologies have one thing in common. They have a passion for what they do. If you find your passion, you can be an innovator, too.

TRULY HISTORIC TRIVIA

- Did you know that when President Barak Obama was inaugurated (sworn in to office) as America's 44th president, there was no iPad?
- Did you know that due to a rubber shortage in WWII, the U.S. government asked scientists to come up with a rubber alternative which was eventually sold to children as Silly Putty?
- Did you know the first African-American woman to receive a patent was Sarah Goode? She invented a folding cabinet bed (1885). Guess you could write and sleep at the same time!
- Do you know the original name of duck tape? It was originally created in 1942 for the military to seal ammunition boxes. Following WWII, people used the versatile tape to connect duct-work in homes and buildings, and called it 'duct' tape.

Tuskegee Airmen in Italy (1945)
Courtesy of the Library of Congress

CHAPTER 20 - EYE-WITNESS TO HISTORY & HEROES
By William Franklin Smith

F or 102 years, Harold Scott Smith, my great-grandpa, eye-witnessed history and heroes. As a person of many words, he loved to organize his memories in journals, letters and (near his last days) on the telephone. He seemed to see each day as a clean sheet of paper on which to record his adventures along the journey called life.

As I was rereading some of his writings, I realized for the first time that he had lived as an American under 22 different presidents. When he was born in July of 1850, Zachary Taylor was president. And when he left us in 1952, Eisenhower was president. Oddly enough, both of those men were heroes of different wars.

Great-grandpa always had a love-hate feeling toward war. As an 11 year old, he wanted to be in the Civil War. But along the many miles, he developed a dislike of the paths that would require so many to give so much. However, his love of country never wavered regardless of the cost. All in all, my great-grandpa had a pretty incredible life. He had the chance to watch a young America grow up while he grew up, himself. His gift of writing is a legacy he left us all and has provided us a chance to witness history through his warm and witty words. Somehow he knew just how to share the stories that would capture the exact moment in time. His storytelling skills will never be matched, but perhaps a bit of it will continue to pass down from Smith to Smith.

Perhaps this book will help you to want to find out more about your own family history (genealogy). Great-grandpa always said that your family history gives you roots and helps you understand who you are and where you came from. Recording our family history gives us a way to share family memories and stories. Now that there are so many ways to take photos and record interviews, the research is unlimited. (At the end of this book is a "My Family Tree and Me" Project, if you want to learn more.)

Hey, let me share the email that just popped up on my computer from Anne, my granddaughter on the USS Lincoln.

Email from Anne H. Smith to William F. Smith

July 12, 2013   9:01 pm

Dear Grandpa,

Happy 81st Birthday to you! We are currently in Virginia and enjoying the time in our home port. Sometimes I find it hard to believe that Great-great-great-grandpa served with President Lincoln, and now I am serving on the USS *Lincoln*. The care package from dad and mom did not last long, as it contained my favorite oatmeal raisin cookies! Take care and will "email" soon.

Love,

Anne

Well, before I sign off, I wanted to review a few of the leaders and heroes Great-grandpa walked with during his life. First off, most of you will recall that his best friend, William Johnston, was the second person to ever receive the Medal of Honor (and the youngest ever). I'm sure his greatest hero would be President Lincoln. His admiration for President Lincoln and the many dark days of war and seeing those dead and wounded just made him respect him more.

He didn't often talk about all those he met in World War II, but one group of fellow Americans he spoke of fondly were the Tuskegee Airmen. He loved their willingness to prove their love of country regardless of how they were treated. He always said America was only as strong as 'we the people' united together. A connection he made with this group of Americans was his own beloved state of South Carolina. If you are ever down in Walterboro, there is a monument dedicated to them near the airport. During World War II, the Walterboro Army Airfield served as a training ground for a group of Tuskegee Airmen. This monument celebrates the courage, dedication and successes of African-American Pilots that fought during World War II.

Great-grandpa was an ordinary person who did extraordinary things. He was never one to praise himself, but he truly did do much to make our lives extraordinary. He would be happy to see the many changes in our country and those citizens who continue to live the American dream, one story at a time. So, from soldier to storyteller, Great-grandpa's story will continue to be told wherever we go. He loved this quote which shows both his and Lincoln's sense of humor, "I'm sorry I wrote such a long letter. I did not have the time to write a short one."

Thanks for reading and for sharing the memories.

William Franklin Smith (2013)

"ME & MY FAMILY" WRITING PROJECT

This project incorporates History and Writing into a fun way to learn your family's genealogy. Researching and recording the generations of a family is called GENEALOGY! When those generations are put into a chart, that chart is called a family tree.

The best place to start is with the oldest members of your family (like grandparents or aunts and uncles). Ask them what they know about their parents and grandparents, and WRITE IT DOWN. One day, future generations of your family may research what you've recorded about your family tree.

Project should include:

- Family Descendant's Form (next page)
- Favorite Family Story
- Favorite Family Photographs

DESCENDANTS OF

Name   **Birth Year**

Primary Sources and Websites

PatriotsPoint.org

library.sc.edu/blogs/newspaper

House.gov (US House of Representatives)

Senate.gov (US Senate)

Whitehouse.gov

Whitehousehistory.org (White House Historical Society)

History.com (History Channel)

AmericanMinute.com

Kids.Clerk.House.gov (House Clerk/DC)

USA.gov

Kids.gov

AOC.gov (Architect of US Capitol)

NPS.gov (National Parks)

LOC.gov (Library of Congress)

Bensguide.gpo.gov (US Government for Kids)

NASA.gov

Thomas.loc.gov (How laws are made)

Archives.gov (National Archives)

MORE FAMILY STORIES

A TRIP THROUGH THE CANAL
By Andrew Harold Smith

G randpa was an ordinary person who did extraordinary things. He was never one to bring glory to himself but led by his example of hard work and a love of God and country. I think he would be happy to see the many changes in our country and to see those who continue to push toward the American Dream. Some have told me that I have grandpa's gift of writing, so I hope you will enjoy my story in print.

Grandpa said that on the date of my birth, January 30, 1900, my lungs worked very well. He said my first cry was as if I had been holding my breath for 9 months and was ready to exhale. My grandpa's tradition was to place a flag in our infant hands as the first thing we held. Do you know how many stars were on our flag in 1900? If you guessed 45, you are correct!

As you can probably tell, my grandpa was my hero. He loved to fish, and we often fished in the Santee River near our family cabin in Cordesville, South Carolina. When we weren't fishing, we were hunting in the nearby Francis Marion Forest. The grave of Francis Marion, nicknamed the "Swamp Fox," is located nearby. He was famous for outwitting the British during the American Revolution! (His guerilla warfare techniques severely crippled British campaigns in the South and helped to ensure American victory in the War for Independence.)

When Grandpa was traveling or gone to war, he always wrote long letters filled with such descriptive words. I felt as if I was standing right beside him. His love of keeping journals and newspaper clippings gave me insight into many things I might never see and places I might never go.

In our family it was always a big event when one of us turned 14. So, on my 14th birthday, my grandpa allowed me to join him in Panama for the PANAMA CANAL'S GRAND OPENING on August 15, 1914. You may remember from reading that he helped build the canal. So, join me on my journey from South Carolina to the Panama Canal, and bring your imagination, too.

It wasn't an easy trip, but there was so much to see, hear and taste. I did not sleep until my eyes could stay open no longer. My Ma packed me a knapsack for when I got hungry along the way, but my appetite hardly had time to catch up with my excitement.

The first part of my journey was by train. From my earliest days, I heard plenty of train tales about various people my Grandpa met working on the railroad. Trains were used to connect all parts of our country in its early days. We learned an old song, which all of us loved back in the day, called "I've been working on the railroad." Sometimes, I can still hear the family bellowing out the words in my head, as if we were all together.

The second part of my trip to reach the Panama Canal was by ship, which took about two weeks. Travelling by ship is very different from traveling by train. Leaving from the port in New York allowed me to see one of the true treasures given to us by the French as a symbol of friendship. The Statue of Liberty stands proudly at 305 feet tall from the ground to the torch. New York Harbor was chosen as the perfect location for her, because it was "where people get their first view of the New World." As a universal symbol of freedom, the statue welcomes all immigrants to America. Just like me, she traveled by ship, but she was in 350 individual pieces packed into 214 crates! Thanks, France for the gift of friendship in the form of our wonderful "Lady Liberty."

On our ship, there were often days we saw nothing but water, waves and darkness. To stay busy, we shared stories, read books, sang songs and even had dancing contests. Oh, and sometimes there were cats aboard ships to keep some other four legged things away. YIKES!

Each crew member had a different responsibility on a ship. The navigator, for instance, used charts and mathematical formulas that kept us from hazards like rocks and shallow water called shoals. He also used an instrument called a sextant. It was a tool used to measure the angle of the stars or sun above the horizon. Every day at noon, the navigator let me help him determine the position of the ship using the sextant.

I sure am grateful I learned about latitude and longitude. Now, when I stare at the stars and the big bright moon, they have more meaning to me. Sometimes I would imagine living somewhere up there beyond those stars, but that probably can never happen!

During the day, we often spotted dolphins and other playful creatures. We would watch them for hours from the bow (front of the ship.) One day, we counted twelve dolphins! They chased each other and jumped right in front of us. At times, they seemed to challenge us to race them through the crashing waves.

At the time, I did not know that the ship on which I travelled would have a place in history. The USS Ancon was the first ship to go through the Panama Canal! There were lots of important people on the ship for this historic event. There were guests of the Secretary of War, U.S. military officers and other officials. Once we arrived, over two hundred people joined us to be aboard the first ship to travel the Panama Canal.

In the midst of the crowd, there was my grandpa eagerly waiting to board our ship, too. It was so wonderful to see his weather-worn face and hear his voice yelling, "Happy Birthday, Andrew!"

Once everyone was aboard, we entered the crowded waterways to receive salutes from the other ships in the crowded harbor. We swung into the channel and headed south toward the Gatun Locks. The date was August 15, 1914. The trip was one of the smoothest made with no problems or delays on that first day.

Believe it or not, the trip took almost ten hours to travel through the canal. But it went by quickly, as I shared the time with my grandpa, sailing through the historic passage. Some reports estimated that there were about two thousand spectators along the channel. On this day, the dreams and plans of four centuries and many years of backbreaking work had finally paid off.

Nothing could really prepare me for moving through the amazing Panama Canal. First, our ship sailed into the open lock from the Atlantic Ocean. Then the chamber closed. As it filled with water, our ship rose to the top - sort of like placing a toy boat in a bathtub. The Panama Canal system of locks allows ships to ascend and descend in steps, like a staircase. There are three upward steps and three downward steps. The canal actually saved ships 8,000 miles of travel and lots of time and money. At the end of the day, we had traveled from the Atlantic Ocean to the Pacific Ocean!

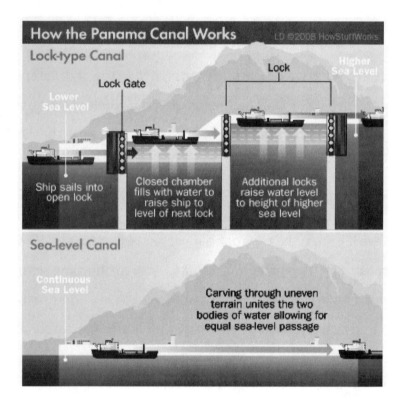

My grandpa said that Teddy Roosevelt was the one who pushed for America's involvement in building the "Big Ditch," as it was often called. He stated that it was President Roosevelt's most important foreign affairs project during his time in the White

House. His philosophy of "Speak softly and carry a big stick" was definitely practiced on this major development, which provided a short cut from the Atlantic to the Pacific Oceans for all countries.

The day was not as joyful as had been planned, however. News was spreading quickly of a war in Europe! That news would later affect me, since it was the start of WWI - "The Great War." Ironically, just like my Grandpa, I would end up defending my country at the age of 16. (Everyone thought I was older, and they did not ask for proof back then!)

Parris Island, WWI and a Medal of Honor Recipient (1916-1919)

My family was not the type to just read about history. They also liked to make history. So, my decision to join the Marines was fully supported by my family. Back in the day, we did not have to prove our age. They assumed I was eighteen. So, like my grandpa, I went in the military earlier than many. I was sixteen when I entered training at Parris Island, SC.

We arrived at Yemassee (a small city near Beaufort) and then took a train to Port Royal (another little town) where we were conveyed to Parris Island by boat to be quarantined. Cleanliness and personal hygiene were stressed and Marines were said to be not only the "first to fight" but also the "first to clean." (All those days as a kid having to clean up came in handy!)

We were being trained for what was going to be "The Great War" (World War I). Eighty percent of all recruits trained at Parris Island to become "Yanks." Our training lasted for eight lo-o-ong weeks. We began with instruction and drills, physical exercise (very physical), swimming, bayonet fighting, personal combat, wall climbing and rope climbing, too!

During our final weeks, we perfected our skills, learned boxing and wrestling, and worked on guard duties. Finally, in the last three weeks, we practiced marksmanship. (If you became a marksman, you could earn up to $5 more per paycheck.)

You probably remember from your studies that, when World War I broke out, the United States maintained a policy of isolationism. (We avoided conflict while trying to negotiate peace between the warring nations). However, when a German U-boat sank the British liner Lusitania in 1915 with 128 Americans onboard, President Woodrow Wilson demanded an end to attacks on passenger ships. Germany complied, and Wilson unsuccessfully tried to mediate a settlement. He repeatedly warned that the U.S. would not tolerate unrestricted submarine warfare, as it was in violation of international law.

My battalion, the 6th Machine Gun Battalion, was chosen to go for extensive training at Quantico, Virginia after our graduation from Parris Island. Pillbox construction (a fort made of concrete), trench warfare techniques and learning to be able to identify the different types of weapons were some of the requirements we had to pass before heading to the "Great War." Pictured below is a pillbox. Can you see me?

We guys thought that trench warfare was just a lot of deep ditches that we had to dig to get to the other side. However, we soon learned that this system of ditches would save our lives, once we got over to France.

The advancement in artillery (weapons) improved greatly during these years. Some even had hydraulic mechanisms for absorbing recoil, so they no longer had to be repositioned after every shot. We could fire more quickly, too. The shells (originally called bombshells) contained explosives, a warhead, and a timing device. They could be directed at the enemy more rapidly, more accurately, and at greater range than anything seen before.

In training, we worked mostly with a Lewis gun or automatic machine gun. It was an American designed weapon and could shoot five to six hundred rounds per minute. Once we arrived at St. Nazaire on Dec. 28, 1917, our familiar Lewis Guns were replaced with the new Hotchkiss M1914 Machine Guns used by the French. Though said to be a better gun, it weighed almost double what the Lewis weighed. Eventually we figured out how to mount these guns to jeeps, tanks and even airplanes, which worked even better for our defense.

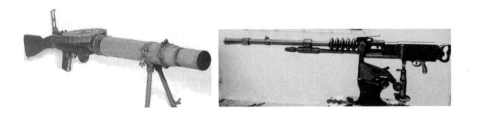

Lewis Light Machine Gun and Hotchkiss M1914 Machine Gun

As the technology of weaponry improved, so did our chances of winning battles. Machine guns were even added to warships as a useful addition to naval armaments. Progress is amazing whether in war or peace. Little would I have ever thought those days Pa and Grandpa taught me how to shoot would help me defend our country clear over in France!

The fighting was fierce, and we were deployed to support the defensive operations in the Chateau–Thierry Sector. We were to provide concentrated fire support at key points along the Allied line. Our job was to lay down covering and harassing fire during both defensive and offensive operations. We were responsible for helping drive through an area called Belleau Wood. Sadly, our commanding officer was mortally wounded during this conflict. It was here that a shell burst near me and knocked me unconscious. When I awoke, the battalion medic was wrapping my left leg and encouraging me to drink some of his famous liquid cure-all for the pain. From this point on, I walked with a reminder that "freedom isn't free."

Leadership skills are often discovered in the heat of the battle, when heroism rises to the surface. The aggressiveness and teamwork of our battalion during the Battle of Belleau Wood earned us great esteem from the French serving in the trenches opposite us. In recognition of our achievements during the fighting, the woods were later renamed the *Bois de la Brigade de*

Marine (French for "the Wood of the Marine Brigade"). In addition, the United States Marine Corps received its nickname "Devil Dogs" as a result of this battle. In recognition of their bravery and accomplishments, the 5th and 6th Marine Regiments and 6th Machine Gun Battalion were awarded the French Croix de Guerre three times!

In August, after a brief rest, our battalion arrived at Camp Bois de L' Eveque on August18, 1918. Here, we went through more intensive training on our machine guns. Practicing with our weapons and conducting drills were things we did over and over. It became second nature, and we could do it in our sleep. Our training had us well, but we also realized the enemy had been preparing, too.

We joined other companies of Marines, as we pressed forward through muddy trenches to our final battle in early November along the Meuse River. As the Germans were pushed back pontoon bridges were hastily erected so we could cross the river. However, before we crossed, the Armistice (an agreement made by opposing sides to stop fighting) brought an end to the war!

My battalion and the 4th Marine Brigade (a small number of infantry battalions and/or other units) were assigned to occupy the area. Military occupation was basically guarding a particular territory of land by troops.

In July 1919, we received our orders to transfer back to the United States. Ten days later, we boarded trains that transported us to the port to head home. From there, we crossed the Atlantic Ocean aboard the Santa Paula. After a little over three weeks, we passed my favorite symbol of freedom – "Lady Liberty!"

The bond of friendship between the United States and France was something I understand more, having fought with them for freedom on their soil, too. Somehow on this day, I felt more free than I had ever experienced and even prouder to be an American! Grandpa's love of our country echoed in my mind and grew in my heart.

TRULY HISTORIC TRIVIA

Did you know there were eight South Carolinians who received the Medal of Honor for "going above and beyond the call of duty" during WWI? One of them was Freddie Stowers from Sandy Springs (near Anderson).

Sadly, on September 28, 1918, just six weeks before the end of World War I, Corporal Freddie Stowers, age 21, was killed leading Company C of the 371st Infantry Regiment into no-man's land to capture German positions. After feigning surrender, the Germans opened up with machine gun and mortar fire, instantly destroying over half of Company C. Stowers rallied the men and led them to knock out one machine gun nest. Though mortally wounded, he urged them on to capture a second trench line, stopping the threat and causing heavy enemy casualties. He is buried, along with 133 of his comrades, at the Meuse-Argonne American Cemetery and Memorial.

Notes